GRANDPA NICK THE CONDUCTOR

GRANDPA NICK THE CONDUCTOR

Mrs. Lynda M. Daniele, O.P.

ReadersMagnet, LLC

I dedicate this little book to the strength of gentleness
and the
goodness of compassion.

The Holy Spirit is always with us!
Can you find Him throughout the book?

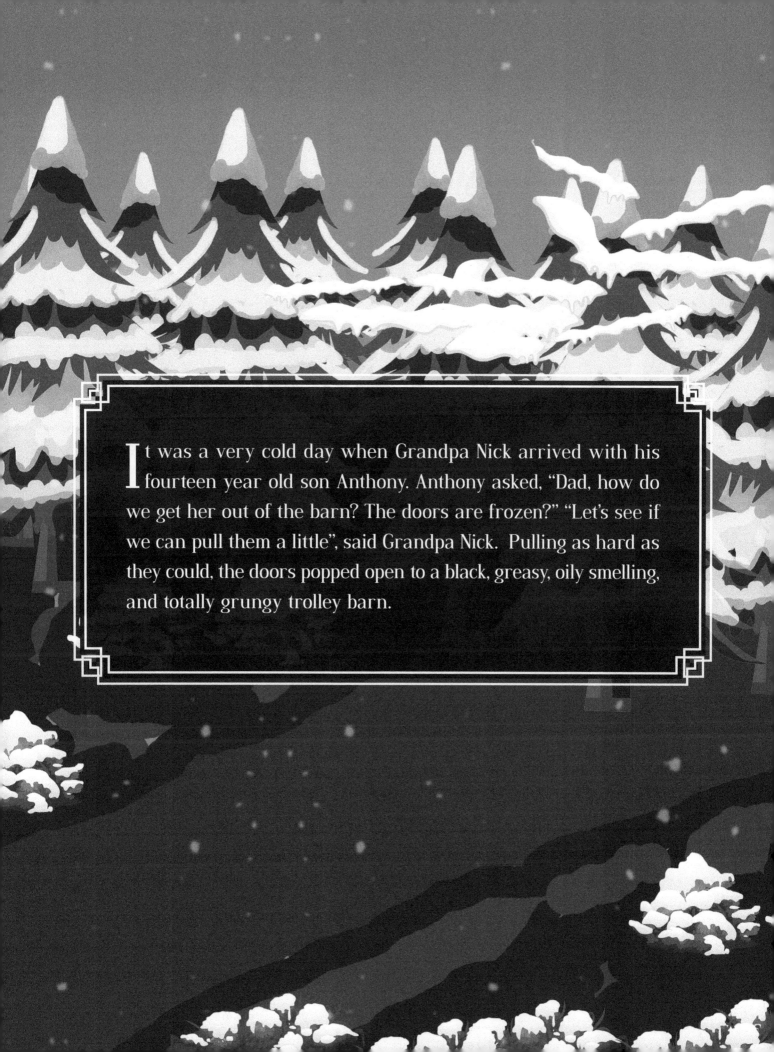

It was a very cold day when Grandpa Nick arrived with his fourteen year old son Anthony. Anthony asked, "Dad, how do we get her out of the barn? The doors are frozen?" "Let's see if we can pull them a little", said Grandpa Nick. Pulling as hard as they could, the doors popped open to a black, greasy, oily smelling, and totally grungy trolley barn.

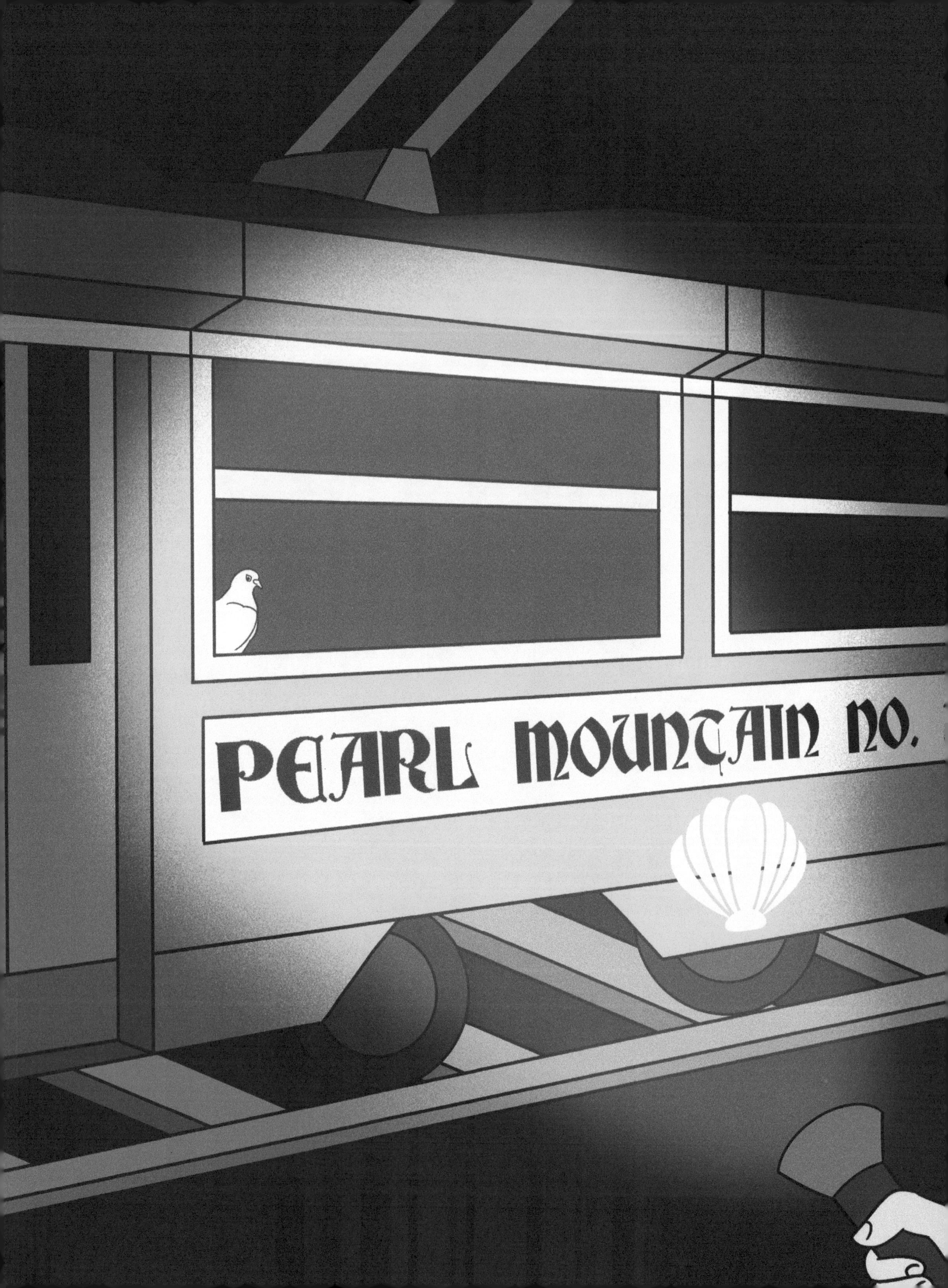
PEARL MOUNTAIN NO.

Grandpa Nick, using his trusty flashlight, made his way to the back of the barn. In the corner his flashlight caught sight of a green and gold shiny surface. There were gold letters with black trim saying "Pearl Mountain No. 3". "There's the "Pearl!" Grandpa Nick exclaimed! Anthony found the light switch and turned on the barn lights. He heard scurrying in the corner that startled him a little. "Mice", he thought, and went to help Grandpa Nick.

Grandpa Nick found the large bronze trolley key and hung it in the corner over the break wheel. "Let's not lose that key," Grandpa Nick mumbled to himself.

Again, Anthony heard a scurry in the corner. "That sounds like an awful big mouse to me." "Dad what do you think that sound was?" "I dunno, maybe a rat or something." said Grandpa Nick. "Can you hand me that wrench over there?" "Sure Dad." answered Anthony.

There was a whining cry and Grandpa Nick put down his wrench and said, "Ok, that's it! Where and what are you?" They both whipped out their flashlights and the search began. "Don't trip on the rails Dad," shouted Anthony. Grandpa Nick had big work boots on and he tended to be a bit klutzy.

Again, a scurrying sound and then a startling large "meow"!
"Sounds like a cat to me," whispered Grandpa Nick. Over to his
left, his flashlight caught a glimpse of a white and black tail
wagging quickly back and forth. "She must be so cold," Anthony
said quietly. "It's ok, we won't hurt you," Grandpa Nick said softly,
with a reassuring calmness.

White and black, dirty and with a very skinny body, a cat
emerged from behind a trolley road wheel. They made a bed for
her with a warming light. "She'll die out here if we don't," uttered
Grandpa Nick.

The next day at daybreak, Grandpa Nick and Anthony set out to check on their trolley cat. They also planned on fixing a trolley lamp that had broken glass and needed to be painted. On their way they stopped to buy some cat food, treats and a bale of hay to keep their "trolley cat" clean and warm.

Arriving at the trolley barn, they opened the doors and went to their warming area. There was no cat there. "Where could she have gone?" Anthony inquired. "Maybe she's found a better corner or perhaps she's just taken off," said Grandpa Nick. Anthony was wishing and hoping she would come back soon.

They put the food out and arranged the hay just so. Then they put the warming light a little higher so the hay wouldn't get too hot. Grandpa Nick put an old towel on top of the hay. He told Anthony that at least if she comes back she'll have a warm dry place to sleep.

Grandpa Nick loved animals so much, even more than he loved mechanical machines that go! They fixed the trolley lamp and put a first coat of paint on it and fixed its broken glass. Anthony checked the outside rails for debris on the tracks. "Can't have any fallen trees or rocks on the rails today", thought Anthony.

Out on the rail Anthony saw the cat under a tree. She was curled up in a ball and looked like a black and white Yin Yang symbol that Anthony had learned about in school. "I'll name her Yin," thought Anthony.

The cat began to move and under her in the dirt were four more 'Little Yin's'! She had kittens by the hollow of a tree. "No wonder why you didn't spend last night in the trolley barn!" Anthony sputtered out excitedly.

He grabbed a rag from his pocket. He scooped up the four Little Yin's and put Mama Yin on his shoulder. "Off to the barn with you all!" smiled Anthony.

"Look at what I found Dad", Anthony exclaimed! "This is why she didn't stay in the trolley barn." He told Grandpa Nick that he named her Yin. Then he placed all the baby Yin's in their new bed. Mama Yin got under the warming light and stretched out as if to say, "Thank you for keeping my family safe."

The next morning when Grandpa Nick and Anthony went to the trolley barn, all the little Yin's were still in their new home. Mama Yin was dining on a bowl of cat food. Grandpa Nick said, "I believe she's actually smiling today!"

Grandpa Nick picked up the little kittens and put them under his jacket to keep them warm from the cold December day. Mama Yin jumped in his lap. Grandpa Nick's new little family snuggled in on his chest and purred sweet sounds of contentment. "Guess I'm not getting much work done today, my little ones," Grandpa chuckled.

Over the next few weeks the Little Yin's jumped, scurried, played, pounced, and purred. Mama Yin nursed, caught mice and taught the Little Yin's to hunt. Grandpa Nick and Anthony got a second coat of paint on the trolley lamp and installed the lamp right on the front of the 'The Pearl',

The four Little Yins were getting bigger. Anthony said to Grandpa Nick, "What's going to happen to the Little Yin's, they need homes now? They can't stay in the barn forever." Grandpa Nick had been thinking about this same question for a while now.

Grandpa Nick saw his other conductor friends and asked them if they wanted a kitten. "No thanks" they said, one after another. When Grandpa Nick drove the trolley he asked his passengers, "Would anyone here like a black and white kitten?" "No thanks", they said over and over. Grandpa Nick even asked the shop owners in his neighborhood if they wanted a kitten. They all said no thanks.

Then one day Grandpa Nick had visitors at the trolley barn. They wanted to see what a real trolley barn looked like and how those mechanical machines go. That was Grandpa Nick's favorite question. He would talk and talk and talk a long time about trolleys.

Grandpa Nick asked his new friends, "Would any of you like a black and white kitten?" He introduced them to the four Little Yins while Mama Yin was off hunting. One of the men mentioned that he had four children and perhaps he could take one kitten for them. "I'll have to ask my wife, but I'll get back to you soon," offered the man. "Oh, sure", agreed Grandpa Nick.

A few days later, the gentleman came back with his wife and four children. "Which one do you want to take home kids?" he asked. "This one; that one; oh, this one's for me; no, I want that one!" they all cried out.

"Let's take them all!" they giggled. The husband looked at his wife and the wife looked at her husband. "What do you think?" asked the wife. "Hum… if it will make them happy… I don't see why not." said the husband. "Yippee!" yelled the four children waving their arms and jumping excitedly up and down.

They gathered the four Little Yins up and put them in a box to go to their new home. Grandpa Nick had lollipops in his jacket pocket. As he gave each child a lollipop he asked them, "What are your names so I can tell Mama Yin when she comes back from hunting?"

"My name is Emma. My name is Joseph. My name is Margaret. My name is Sean," they said one by one as they happily got their treat. "Congratulations on your new little family," smiled Grandpa Nick. Mama Yin came back from hunting and noticed that the four Little Yin's were not there. A little sad, she jumped on Grandpa's shoulder and purred a soft purr and then comfortably fell fast asleep.

Over the years Mama Yin stayed with Grandpa Nick. She would always snuggle up on his shoulder while he drove the trolley on his route. All of the passengers loved Mama Yin and Grandpa Nick when they went on trolley rides with them. "We're a good team," Grandpa Nick told the passengers. Many commented on the love between Grandpa Nick and Mama Yin and said that they were a match made in heaven.

Many years later, Grandpa Nick is now in heaven and so is Mama Yin. They're driving a trolley picking up heavenly souls. "All aboard!" bellows Grandpa Nick with Mama Yin on his shoulder. "We'll always make a pretty good team", winked Grandpa Nick, as they sing along their way...

In trolley whistle language -

One whistle means to stop.
Two whistles means to go.
Many short whistles mean danger.
Get your trolley whistle, recorder, trumpet, tambourine and
instruments ready … ♩♩♩♩ (4 for 4 beats)   Play your instruments
on the whistle refrain and RAP!

Trolley Whistle Song

Mrs. Lynda M. Daniele, O.P.

I am the Conductor and we're going on a trip.
I am the Conductor and we're going on a trip. (2 long whistles… means go)
Let's keep going on this beautiful day!
The sun is shining and we're on our way! (2 long whistles… means go)
It's time to stop and let folks off.   (1 long whistle… means stop.)
Let's get going again, let's get going! (2 long whistles… means go)
Oh no there's a bear on the tracks! Danger!
(Many short whistles… means danger!)
He's ok he's moving off the tracks. (2 long whistles… means go)
We're going back to the station. (2 long whistles… means go)
It's time to stop the trolley at our destination. (1 long whistle… means stop)
Hope you had a time that's jolly,
Riding with me on the heavenly trolley!!
(2 long whistles… means go) TA-DA!!!

10620 Treena Street, Suite 230

San Diego, California,

CA 92131 USA

www.readersmagnet.com

1.619.354.2643

CPSIA information can be obtained
at www.ICGtesting.com
Printed in the USA
BVHW020254051021
618136BV00010B/218